This book belongs to...

....

....

The Nursery Collection
Teddy Bear Tales

This is a Parragon Publishing Book
This edition published in 2003

Parragon Publishing, Queen Street House, 4 Queen Street, Bath BA1 1HE, UK

Produced by The Templar Company plc

Copyright © Parragon 2000

Edited by Caroline Repchuk
Designed by Kilnwood Graphics

Printed and bound in China
ISBN 1 40540 220 2

The Nursery Collection
Teddy Bear Tales

p

CONTENTS

BEARS AHOY

One summer's day, three little boys went for a picnic by the bank of a river. They took with them their swimming things, some cheese and tomato sandwiches and, of course, their teddy bears.

When they arrived, they found a small boat tied to a tree. The boys climbed on board, taking their teddies with them, and had a great game of pirates. The boys pretended to walk the plank, and soon they were all splashing about, playing and swimming in the river. They chased each other through the shallow water, and disappeared along the river and out of sight.

Now, the three bears left on board the boat did not get on very well together. Oscar was a small, honey-colored bear. He was good friends with Mabel, who had shaggy brown fur, but neither of them liked Toby. He was bigger than they were and he was a bully. He was always growling at the other bears and telling them what to do.

As soon as the boys were out of sight, Toby leapt to his feet. The boat rocked. Oscar and

Mabel begged him to sit down.

"I'm a fearless sailor," cried Toby. "I've sailed the seven seas and now I'm going to sail them again." He untied the boat, and pushed it away from the bank. The boat lurched from side to side.

"Come on, crew. Look lively!" shouted Toby. "Do as I say or I'll make you walk the plank." Now that it was untied, the little blue boat began to drift. It turned sideways gently, then caught the

10

main current and began to gather speed.

"Toby!" cried Oscar. "We're moving!"

"Of course we are, you big softie," growled Toby. "We're bold and fearless pirates on the high seas."

Oscar and Mabel clung together in fright, as the little boat sailed down the river, past fields and houses. "Help!" they shouted. "Toby, make it stop!" But Toby was having a great time.

"Ha, ha," shouted Toby. "This is the life!"

Oscar glanced over the side. He wished he hadn't. The sight of everything passing by so

quickly made him feel seasick.

"Look out, Toby!" he cried. "We're going to hit the bank. Steer it away."

But Toby did nothing. The boat hit the bank with a thump and Toby fell forward. The boat swung round and headed for the middle of the river once more.

12

"Toby!" shouted Mabel. "Save us!"

But Toby was sitting in the bottom of the boat, rubbing a big bump on his head.

...can't. I don't know how to sail a boat," he whimpered, feebly. He hid his face in his paws and began to cry. The boat zig-zagged on down the river, with the little bears clinging on to the sides in fright. In time, the river became wider and they could hear the cry of seagulls.

"Oh, Toby," cried Mabel. "We're heading for the sea. Do something!"

"Nobody likes me," wailed Toby. "Now we're going to sink to the bottom of the sea, and you won't like me either!"

Oscar wasn't listening. He had found a rope hanging from the sail. "Let's put the sail up and see if it will blow us to shore," he said.

"We'll be blown out to sea," wailed Toby, but Oscar and him, and carried on. The wind fill ar he little boat started moving for right across the bay to the

far side, and blew up on to the beach.

"Oh, Oscar, you are a hero!" sighed Mabel, hugging him tight. "You saved us!"

Imagine the bears' surprise to see the three little boys running towards them along the beach — they had gone to find the coastguard and raise the alarm. There were hugs and kisses all round when they found the bears safe and sound. And you can be sure that from that day on, Toby was a much wiser and kinder bear, and he never bullied the others again.

POOR LITTLE TED

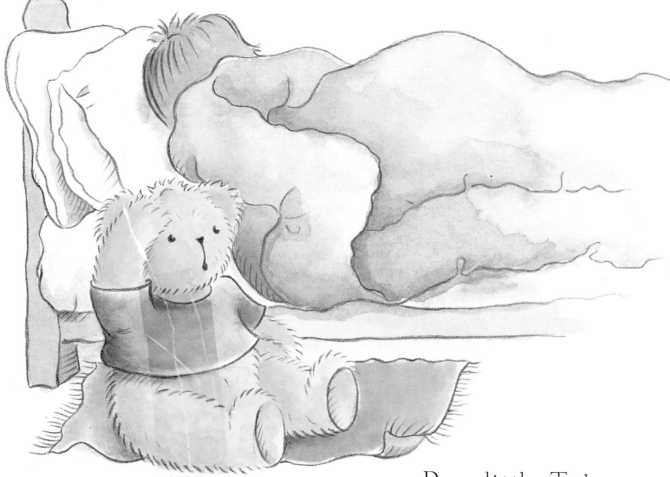

Poor little Ted
Fell out of bed,
And found that he had
A big bump on his head!

He let out a scream,
I woke from my dream,
And soon made him better
With cake and ice cream!

IN A SPIN

I had a little teddy,
He went everywhere with me,
But now I've gone and lost him,
Oh, where can my teddy be?

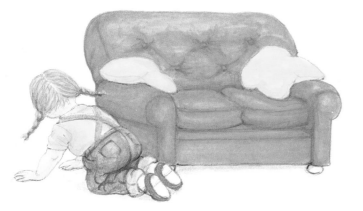

I've looked behind the sofa,
I've looked beneath the bed,
I've looked out in the garden,
And in the garden shed!

I've looked inside the bathtub,
And underneath my chair,
Oh, where, oh, where is Teddy?
I've hunted everywhere!

At last I try the kitchen,
My face breaks in a grin.
There's Teddy in the washtub –
Mom's sent him for a spin!

BARNEY THE BOASTFUL BEAR

Barney was a very boastful bear.

"Look at my lovely soft fur!" he would say to the other toys. "See how it shines!"

Barney loved to talk about himself. "I'm the smartest toy in the playroom!" he would say. "It's a well-known fact."

He didn't know that the other toys all laughed about him behind his back.

"That bear thinks he's so smart," growled Scotty Dog. "But he isn't smart enough to know when everyone's fed up with him!"

"He'll learn his lesson one of these days," said Molly Monkey, and sure enough, that is just what happened...

One hot summer's day, the toys lazed in the warm playroom. "Wouldn't it be lovely if we could go for a walk outside," said Rag Doll.

"We could have a lovely picnic in the woods!" said Old Bear.

"Even better, we could go for a drive in the toy car first!" said Rabbit.

"But none of us is big or clever enough to drive the toy car," said Rag Doll, sadly.

"I am!" came a voice from the corner. It was Barney. He had been listening to them talking.

"I can drive the toy car. And I know the best place for a picnic in the woods," he said.

"We've never seen you drive the car," said Rabbit, suspiciously.

"That's because I drive it at night, when you're asleep," said Barney. "I'm a very good driver, in fact."

"Ooh, let's go then!" cried Rag Doll. And in no time they had packed up a picnic and were sitting ready in the car.

"Er, I don't feel like driving today, actually," mumbled Barney. "It's too hot." But the others

were not interested in hearing excuses, so rather reluctantly Barney climbed into the driver's seat and started the engine. You see, the truth was, Barney had never really driven the car before, and he was scared. But he wanted to show off, so he pretended to know what he was doing.

Off they set down the garden path. "Toot, toot!" Barney beeped the horn as he turned the little car out into the country lane, and soon they were driving along, singing merrily.

All was going well, until Rag Doll suddenly said, "Hey, Barney, didn't we just miss the turning for the woods?"

"I know where I'm going," said Barney, crossly. "Leave it to me." And he made the little car go faster.

"Slow down a bit, Barney!" called Old Bear, from the back seat. "My fur is getting all ruffled." He was starting to feel anxious.

"I don't need a back seat driver, thank you," said Barney, with a growl, and made the car go even faster. By now the others were starting to feel scared, but Barney was having a great time.

"Aren't I a wonderful driver!" he chuckled. "Look – no hands!" And he took his paws off the steering wheel. Just then they reached a sharp corner. The little car went spinning off the side of the road and crashed into a tree, tipping all the toys out into the ditch!

They were a bit dazed, but luckily no one was hurt. They were not pleased with Barney though. "You silly bear!" said Rabbit, crossly. "We could have all been badly hurt!"

"We'll have to walk home now," said Rag Doll, rubbing her head. "Where are we?"

Everyone looked at Barney.

"Don't ask me!" he said, quietly.

"But you said you knew the way!" said Old Bear, indignantly.

"I was only pretending," said Barney, his voice trembling. "I don't really know how to drive, and I don't know where we are!" And he started to cry.

The other toys were furious with Barney.

"You naughty boastful bear!" they scolded. "Now see what trouble your boasting has got us into!"

The lost toys walked through the dark woods all night long, clinging together in fright as shadows loomed around them.

They had never been out at night before. Then just before dawn, they spotted the little house where they lived, and crept back into the playroom.

What a relief it was to be home again!
Luckily their owner had not noticed they
were missing, so she never knew what an
adventure her toys had been having while
she was fast asleep. She often wondered what
had happened to her toy car though.

As for Barney, he was very sorry for the trouble
he had caused. After a while the other toys
forgave him, and from that day on he never
boasted about anything again.

TEA WITH THE QUEEN

Teddy bear, teddy bear,
Where have you been?
I've been up to London to visit the queen!

I went to her palace,
And knocked at the gate,
And one of her soldiers said, please would I wait?

Then one of her footmen,
All dressed in red,
Led me inside, saying, step this way, Ted!

And there in a huge room,
High on her throne,
Sat the poor queen, taking tea all alone.

She said, how delightful,
Sit down, fill your tum!
And soon we were chattering just like old chums!

And when time came to leave,
She shook hands and then,
She said, come back soon, we must do it again!

THE BEAR
WILL HAVE TO GO

While Lucy slept in the shade of a tree, Cuthbert went for a walk into the woods and was soon quite lost. He had no idea which way was back, so he sat down and thought about what to do next.

When Lucy awoke, she looked around in surprise. Her teddy bear, Cuthbert was missing. She thought someone had taken him, for she didn't know that when people are asleep their teddy bears like to go walking.

"Cuthbert!" she called. "Cuthbert, where are you?"

He wasn't very far away. Lucy soon found him sniffing at a clump of moss.

"There you are!" she sighed. "I thought I'd lost you. Where's your waistcoat?"

In fact, Lucy really had lost Cuthbert, for the bear she was now taking home was not a teddy bear at all, but a real baby bear cub! As they ran back through the woods, the bear in Lucy's arms kept very still. He stared straight ahead without blinking, and tried not to sneeze. Soon they were back in Lucy's bedroom. Lucy flung the bear on her bed, then went to run a bath.

"Time to escape!" thought the bear. He slid off the bed, pulling the covers after him. He ran over to the window and tried to climb up the curtains. They tore down and tumbled to a heap on the floor. Just then Lucy's mother came into the room. The bear froze. Then Lucy appeared.

"Look at this mess," said Lucy's mother. "You've been playing with that bear again. Please tidy up."

Lucy had no idea how her room had got in such a mess, but she tidied up, took the bear into the bathroom and put him on the edge of the tub.

"Don't fall in," she said, and went to fetch a towel. The bear jumped into the tub with a great splash. He waved his paws wildly sending sprays of soapy water across the room. When he heard footsteps, he froze and floated on his back in the water as if nothing was wrong. It was Lucy, followed by her mother. "Oh, Lucy! What a mess!"

"Cuthbert must have fallen in," cried Lucy, rubbing his wet fur with a towel.

"A teddy bear couldn't make all this mess on its own," said Lucy's mother. "Please clean it up."

Lucy looked carefully at Cuthbert. Something was different about him, but she just couldn't work out what it was.

That night, while Lucy slept, the bear tip-toed downstairs. He needed to get back to the woods where he belonged, but he was hungry. In the kitchen he found lots of food, and he had a feast.

When Lucy came down for a glass of milk she found him with food all over his paws. The bear froze. Then her mother appeared in the doorway.

"This is the last straw, Lucy," said her mother, crossly. "You have been very naughty today, and every time something happens you've got that bear with you. If there is any more bad behaviour, the bear will have to go."

When her mother had gone back upstairs, Lucy looked carefully at the bear.

"You're not Cuthbert are you?" she said. The bear looked back at her and blinked. Lucy gasped. "You're a real bear!"

Now all the mess made sense! Lucy could hardly believe she had made such a mistake. She stroked the bear gently and he licked her finger.

"I'd better get you back to the woods before there's any more trouble," she said. "And I'd better try to find the real Cuthbert."

So early next morning, before her parents were awake, she crept out of the house carrying the bear. Out in the woods she put the bear on the ground. He licked her hand and padded away.

Lucy was sad to see the little bear go. She wiped a tear from her eye as she turned away... and there at the foot of a tree sat her teddy bear, Cuthbert! Lucy picked him up and hugged him.

"Where have you been?" she asked. "You'll never guess the trouble I've been in. What have you been doing all night?"

Cuthbert said nothing. He just smiled. What had he been doing all night? Well, that's another story!

TEDDY BEARS' PICNIC

Little Bear brought chocolate cake,
Raggy Bear brought honey,
Baby Bear brought ice cream,
With butterscotch all runny!

Tough Old Ted brought cinnamon buns,
Silky Bear brought jello,
Shaggy Bear brought cookies and
Egg sandwiches all yellow!

Woolly Bear brought pecan pie,
Tiny Ted brought candy,
Mrs Bear brought little plates
She thought would come in handy.

Off they set into the woods,
A sunny spot they found,
And had a teddies picnic,
As they shared the goodies round!

LAZY TEDDY

There was nothing Lazy Teddy liked more than to be tucked up snug and warm in Joshua's bed. Every morning the alarm clock would ring and Joshua would leap out of bed and fling open the curtains. "I love mornings!" he'd say, stretching his arms up high as the sun poured in through the window. "You're crazy!" Teddy would mutter, and he'd burrow down beneath the quilt to the bottom of the bed, where he'd spend the rest of the morning snoozing happily.

"Come out and play, you lazy bear," Joshua would call. But Lazy Teddy wouldn't budge. He would just snore even louder.

Joshua wished that Teddy would be more lively, like his other friends' bears. He loved having adventures, but they would be even better if Teddy would share them with him.

One evening, Joshua decided to have a talk with Teddy before they went to bed. He told him all about the fishing trip he'd been on that day with his friends and their teddy bears.

"It was lots of fun, Teddy. I wish you'd been there. It really is time you stopped being such a lazybones. Tomorrow is my birthday, and I'm having a party. There will be games, and presents and ice-cream. Please promise you'll come?"

"It does sound like fun," said Teddy. "Okay, I promise. I'll get up just this once."

The next morning, Joshua was up bright and early. "Yippee, it's my birthday today!" he yelled, dancing round the room. He pulled the covers off his bed. "Come on, Teddy, time to get up!"

"Just five more minutes!" groaned Teddy, and he rolled over and fell straight back to sleep. When Joshua came back up to his room after breakfast, Teddy still wasn't up. Well, by now Joshua was getting quite cross with Teddy. He reached over and poked him in the tummy. Teddy opened one eye and growled. "Wake up, Teddy! You promised, remember?" said Joshua.

Teddy yawned. "Oh, if I must!" he said, and muttering and grumbling he climbed out of bed. He washed his face and paws, brushed his teeth and put on his best red vest.

"There, I'm ready!" he said.

"Good," said Joshua. "About time too!"

Just then the doorbell rang, and Joshua ran to answer it. "I'll come and fetch you in a minute," he said to Teddy. But when he returned there was no sign of Teddy, just a gentle snoring coming from the bottom of the bed.

Joshua was so cross and upset with Lazy Teddy, that he decided to leave him right where he was.

"He'll just have to miss the party!" he said. Deep down though, he was hurt that Teddy wouldn't keep his promise.

Joshua enjoyed his party, although he wished that Teddy had been there. That night when he got into bed, he lay crying quietly into his pillow.

Teddy lay awake in the dark, listening. He knew Joshua was crying because he had let him down, and he felt very ashamed of himself.

"I'm sorry!" whispered Lazy Teddy, and he snuggled up to Joshua and stroked him with a paw until he fell asleep.

The next morning when the alarm clock rang, Joshua leapt out of bed, as usual. But what was this? Teddy had leapt out of bed too, and was stretching his paws up high. Joshua looked at him in amazement.

"What are we doing today, then?" asked Teddy.

"G...g...going for a picnic," stammered Joshua, in surprise. "Are you coming?"

"Of course," said Teddy. And from that day on, Teddy was up bright and early every day, ready to enjoy another day of adventures with Joshua, and he never let him down again.

WOBBLY BEAR

Mr and Mrs Puppety owned an old-fashioned toy shop. They made toys by hand in a room at the back of the shop. But they were getting old and their eyesight was bad.

"It's time we got an apprentice toymaker," said Mr Puppety to his wife. They soon found a young lad called Tom to work for them. He worked hard and carefully. He spent his first week making a teddy bear. When he had finished he showed the bear to Mr and Mrs Puppety.

"He looks very cuddly," said Mrs Puppety.

Tom was pleased that they liked his bear and he went off home whistling happily.

"He is a lovely bear," said Mr Puppety, "but his head is a bit wobbly."

"I know," said his wife, "but it's Tom's first try. Let's just put him up there on the shelf with the other teddy bears."

That night Wobbly Bear sat on the shelf and started to cry. He had heard what Mr and Mrs Puppety had said about him.

"What's wrong?" asked Brown Bear, who was sitting next to him.

"My head is wobbly," sobbed Wobbly Bear.

"Does it hurt?" asked Brown Bear.

"No," replied Wobbly Bear.

"Then why are you crying?" asked Brown Bear.

"Because nobody will want to buy a wobbly bear. I'll be left in this shop forever and nobody will ever take me home and love me," he cried.

"Don't worry," said Brown Bear. "We've all got our faults, and you look fine to me. Just try your best to look cute and cuddly and you'll soon have someone to love you." This made Wobbly Bear feel much happier and he soon fell fast asleep.

The next day the shop was full of people, but nobody paid any attention to Wobbly Bear. Then a little boy looked up at the shelf and cried, "Oh, what a lovely bear. Can I have that one, Daddy?"

Wobbly Bear's heart lifted as the little boy's daddy reached up to his shelf. But he picked up Brown Bear instead and handed him to the little boy. Wobbly Bear felt sadder than ever. Nobody wanted him. All of his new friends would get sold and leave the shop, but he would be left on the shelf gathering dust. Poor old Wobbly Bear!

Now, Mr and Mrs Puppety had a little grand-daughter called Jessie who loved to visit the shop and play with the toys. All the toys loved her because she was gentle and kind. It so happened that the next time she came to visit it was her birthday, and her grandparents told her she could choose any toy she wanted as her present.

"I know she won't choose me," thought Wobbly Bear sadly. "Not with all these other beautiful toys to choose from."

53

But to Wobbly's amazement, Jessie looked up and pointed at his shelf and said, "I'd like that wobbly bear please. No one else will have a bear quite like him."

Mr Puppety smiled and gave Wobbly to Jessie. She hugged and kissed him, and Wobbly felt so happy he almost cried. She took him home and put a smart red bow around his neck ready for her birthday party. He felt very proud indeed.

Soon the other children arrived, each carrying their teddy bears under their arms.

Wobbly Bear could not believe his eyes when he saw the little boy with his friend Brown Bear!

"I'm having a teddy bears' picnic," Jessie explained to him, hugging him tight. All of the children and the bears had a wonderful time, especially Wobbly. He had found a lovely home, met his old friend and made lots of new ones.

"See, I told you not to worry," said Brown Bear.

"I know," said Wobbly. "And I never will again."

GEE UP, TEDDY

Gee up, Teddy,
Don't you stop!
Ride on the
hobbyhorse,
Clippety clop!
Clippety clopping,
Round and round.
Giddy up,
We're toybox bound!

THREE TEDS IN A TUB

Rub-a-dub, dub,
Three teds in a tub,
Sailing across the sea!
But the rumble of tums,
And the smell of hot buns,
Will bring them back home for tea!

GREEDY BEAR

If there is one thing in the whole wide world that a teddy bear likes more than anything it is buns — big sticky cinnamon buns with sugary tops, and squishy middles. A teddy bear will do almost anything for a bun. But for one greedy little teddy bear called Clarence, sticky buns were to be his unsticking!

Rag Doll baked the most wonderful buns in the little toy cooker. She baked big buns and small buns, iced buns and raisin buns, cinnamon buns and poppy-seed buns, and even hot-cross buns! She shared them out amongst the toys in the playroom, and everybody loved them. But no-one loved them as much as Clarence.

"If you will give me your bun, I'll polish your boots!" he'd say to Tin Soldier.

And sometimes if Tin Soldier was not feeling too hungry, he'd agree. There was always someone who would give Clarence their bun in return for a favor, and sometimes Clarence would eat five or six buns in one day!

Then he'd be busy washing the dolls' dresses, brushing Scotty Dog's fur, or cleaning the toy policeman's car. He would even stand still and let the clown throw custard pies at him!

So you see, Clarence was not a lazy bear, but he was a greedy bear, and in spite of all his busyness, he was becoming a rather plump little greedy bear. All those buns were starting to show around his middle, and his fur was beginning to strain at the seams!

Then one day Clarence rushed into the playroom full of excitement. His owner, Penny, had told him that next week she was taking him on a teddy bears' picnic.

"She says there will be honey sandwiches and

ice cream and cookies — and lots and lots of buns!"
Clarence told the others, rubbing his hands
together. "I can hardly wait! In fact all this
excitement has made me hungry, so I think I'll
have a bun." And he took a big sticky bun out
from under a cushion where he'd hidden it earlier.

"Oh, Clarence!" said Rabbit. "One of these days
you will simply go pop!"

"Just be happy I don't like carrots!" said
Clarence with a smile.

Well, that week Clarence was busier than ever. Every time he thought about the picnic it made him feel hungry, and then he'd have to find someone who'd let him have their bun. He ate bun after bun, and would not listen when Rag Doll warned him that his back seam was starting to come undone.

The day of the teddy bears' picnic dawned, and Clarence yawned and stretched, smiling to himself with excitement. But as he stretched he felt a strange popping sensation all down his stomach. He tried to sit up in bed, but to his alarm he found he could not move. He looked down to see that the seams around his tummy had popped open, and his stuffing was spilling out all over the bed!

"Help!" he cried. "I'm exploding!"

Just then, Penny woke up. "Oh, Clarence!" she cried when she saw him. "I can't take you to the teddy bears' picnic like that!"

Penny showed Clarence to her mommy, who said he would have to go to the toy hospital.

Clarence was away from the playroom for a whole week, but when he came back he was as good as new. Some of his stuffing had been taken out, and he was all sewn up again.

He had had lots of time to think in the hospital about what a silly greedy bear he had been. How he wished he had not missed the picnic. The other teddies said it was the best day out they had ever had. Penny had taken Rabbit instead.

"It was terrible," moaned Rabbit. "Not a carrot in sight. I did save you a bun though." And he pulled a big sticky bun out of his pocket.

"No thank you, Rabbit," said Clarence. "Funnily enough, I've gone off buns!"

Of course, Clarence did not stop eating buns for long, but from then on he stuck to one a day. And he still did favors for the others, only now he did them for free!

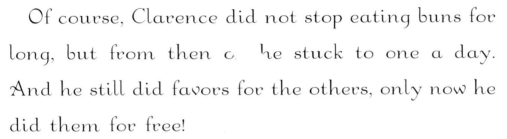

TEN LITTLE TEDDIES

Ten little teddies, standing in a line,
One of them went fishing, so then there were nine.

Nine little teddies, marching through a gate,
One stopped to tie his shoe, so then there were eight.

Eight little teddies, floating up in heaven,
One fell down and broke his crown,
so then there were seven.

Seven little teddies, doing magic tricks,
One made himself disappear, so then there were six.

Six little teddies, about to take a dive,
One of them was scared of heights, so then there were five.

Five little teddies, running on the shore,
One went surfing in the waves, so then there were four.

Four little teddies, eating cakes for tea,
One of them was feeling sick, so then there were three.

Three little teddies, heading for the zoo,
One of them hopped on a bus, so then there were two.

Two little teddies, playing in the sun,
One of them got sunburnt, so then there was one.

One little teddy, who's had lots of fun,
It's time for him to go to sleep, so now there are none.

TOUGH TED
LOSES HIS GROWL

The alarm clock started to ring and Katie jumped out of bed, bursting with energy. Tough Ted opened one sleepy eye (which was all he could do, as the other one had fallen off years ago) and stretched.

"Another morning," he yawned. "I don't suppose it will be a good one."

Tough Ted was a very old bear. He had belonged to Katie's mom when she was young. He had been a smart teddy then, and happy, but now he was in a sorry state and was always grumpy. He was the oldest of the toys and he had been through some tough times. The other toys loved him, but they were fed up with his constant moaning and groaning.

"When is this bed going to be made? I can't get comfortable with all these covers thrown back!" he complained. "And they should pull that blind down, the sun's shining straight into my eye," he grumbled.

"Talking of which, it's about time they gave me a new one," he moaned. He carried on growling all morning.

"If he doesn't stop complaining soon I'm going to stuff my hat in his mouth," whispered Soldier to Clown as they sat on the shelf.

"Not if I put my ju___ balls in there first!" said Clown. All the toys giggle___

"It's about time we taught ___," said Rag Doll. "What can we do to stop ___aning?"

"What about sticking a band-aid over his mouth while he's asleep?" twittered Owl, who was always wise.

"That's a brilliant idea, Owl!" said Rag Doll, and everyone agreed.

So that night, Rag Doll fetched a band-aid from the bathroom cabinet, and stuck it firmly over Tough Ted's mouth while he was asleep. All the toys were delighted – peace and quiet at last!

The next morning the alarm went off and Katie went into the bathroom. Tough Ted opened his eye and was just about to moan that the alarm was still ringing, when he realized he could not open his mouth!

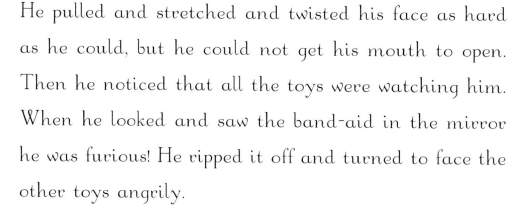

He pulled and stretched and twisted his face as hard as he could, but he could not get his mouth to open. Then he noticed that all the toys were watching him. When he looked and saw the band-aid in the mirror he was furious! He ripped it off and turned to face the other toys angrily.

"Who did this?" he bellowed. "When I find out who it was, there'll be trouble, growwwll! Have you no respect for an old bear?" He went on and on and on. He grew red in the face, and looked terribly cross. All the toys became quite scared.

Then, as he was growling at the top of his voice, a funny thing happened. His voice began to crack. He tried to clear his throat, but it was no use. He had lost his voice completely!

"Well it serves you right!" said Rag Doll. "All you do is moan, moan, moan, and we're tired of listening to you. We put the band-aid on your mouth to teach you a lesson. But now you've moaned so much that you've made yourself lose your voice completely."

With that a big tear rolled down Tough Ted's cheek. He was not so tough after all. He had not realized that he moaned so much, and he felt very sorry.

Rag Doll did not like seeing Tough Ted so sad. All the toys felt a bit guilty for what they had done.

"I'll go and get you some honey from the kitchen," said Rag Doll. "It will soothe your throat. But you must promise not to start moaning again."

After Rag Doll had given Tough Ted a spoonful of honey, he whispered, "I'm sorry. I promise I'll try not to moan any more. I didn't realise I'd become such a grumpy old bear."

With that, all the toys gave Tough Ted a hug and Rag Doll gave him some more honey.

Since then Tough Ted has tried really hard not to moan. But whenever he does, he thinks about the band-aid and quickly stops himself before anyone hears! And the rest of the toys do their best to look after him and keep him happy.

MIDNIGHT FUN

Just as midnight's striking,
When everyone's asleep,
Teddies yawn and stretch and shake,
And out of warm beds creep.

They sneak out from their houses,
And gather in the dark,
Then skip along the empty streets,
Heading for the park.

And there beneath the moonlight,
They tumble down the slides,
They swoosh up high upon the swings,
And play on all the rides.

And when the sun comes peeping,
They rush home to their beds,
And snuggle down as children wake,
To cuddle with their teds!

THE NAUGHTY BEARS

One sunny summer's day, Ben and Fraser's parents told them to pack their things, as they were going to the beach.

"Yippee!" said Ben. "Can we take our teddies?"

"As long as you keep an eye on them," said Daddy. "We don't want to spend all afternoon looking for them if you lose them again!"

Ben and Fraser took their teddies everywhere they went, but they were always losing them, and then there was a great hunt to find them. But the truth was, that when no one was looking, the naughty little teddies would run away in search of excitement and adventure.

Today was no different. The family arrived at the beach and unpacked their things. Daddy sat reading a newspaper and Mommy took out a book. Soon Ben and Fraser were busy building sandcastles. When the naughty teddies saw that no one was looking, they jumped up and ran away giggling, all along the beach.

"Let's go exploring," said Billy, who was the oldest bear. "I can see a cave over there." He pointed to a dark hole in the rocks close to the water.

"It looks a bit dark and scary," said Bella.

"Don't be silly," said Billy. "You're a bear. Bears like dark caves!"

The little bears clambered over the rocks and into the cave. It was very deep, and very dark. Just then, Bella spotted something gleaming on the floor. She picked it up and showed it to Billy.

"Gold!" said Billy, in excitement, taking the little coin from Bella. "This must be a smuggler's cave! Maybe the smugglers are still here. Let's take a look!"

"No!" said Bella. "They could be dangerous. Let's go back." She turned and ran back outside, where she saw to her horror that while they had been exploring the tide had come in, and cut the rocks off from the beach.

"Billy!" she called. "Come quick, we're stranded!"

Meanwhile, Ben and Fraser had finished making sandcastles and found that their teddy bears were missing.

"Oh, no," groaned Daddy. "Not again!"

The family hunted high and low along the beach, but there was no sign of the bears to be found. "Maybe they've been washed out to sea," said Fraser, his voice trembling at the thought.

Back at the cave the naughty teddies could see their owners looking for them. They jumped up and down and waved their paws. "It's no use," said Bella, "they can't see us. We're too small."

"Don't worry," said Billy, trying to sound braver than he felt.

Just then, two men appeared from the other side of the rocks. The teddies froze – these must be the smugglers! They trembled in fear as the men picked them up, clambered over the rocks, and tossed them into a little boat that had been hidden from view. The teddies clung together at the bottom of the boat as the men jumped in and began to row. Where were they taking them?

82

After a while, the boat stopped and one of the men jumped out. He grabbed the bears and held them in the air high above his head, calling out, "Has anyone lost these bears?"

Everyone on the beach looked up, and Ben and Fraser raced over and grabbed their bears.

"Thank you," said Daddy. "We've been looking everywhere for them."

"We found them up by that cave," said one of the men, pointing over to the cave. "Your kids must have left them there."

"But they've been here building sandcastles all afternoon..." said Daddy, looking puzzled.

No one ever did find out how the naughty teddies got to the cave, or where the little coin in Billy's pocket came from. But from then on Daddy said they had to stay at home. The naughty teddies didn't really mind. They'd had enough adventures for the time being. And it gave them lots of time to play their favorite game – hide and seek!

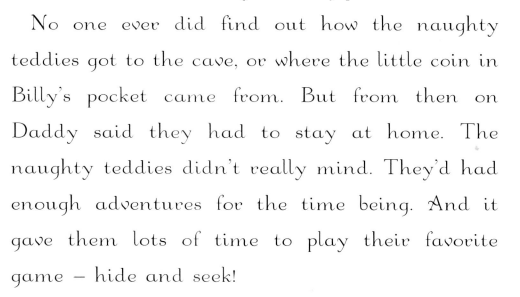

MY BEST FRIEND

He cuddles me at bedtime,
And keeps me safe at night,
If I have a bad dream,
And wake up in a fright.

He is my constant playmate,
And often shares my tea,
He always lets me win at games,
And has a smile for me.

He shares in all my secrets,
And never shows surprise,
He listens to my problems,
With kindness in his eyes.

And when I'm feeling lonely,
On him I can depend,
He's more than just a teddy,
He is my best, best friend!

SOME TEDDY BEARS

Some teddy bears are tiny,
Some teddy bears are tall,
Some teddy bears are big and round,
And some teddy bears are small.

Some teddy bears are woolly,
Some teddy bears are rough,
Some teddy bears have shaggy fur,
And some are balls of fluff.

Some teddy bears look happy
Some teddy bears look sad,
Some teddy bears are very good,
And some teddy bears are bad.

But all teddy bears are loyal,
And all teddy bears are true,
And all teddy bears need lots of love
And hugs from me and you.

TEDDY BEAR TEARS

"Boo hoo! I want to go home!"

As a little fairy called Mavis flew past the garbage dump, holding her nose, she heard an unmistakeable sound coming from the other side of a very smelly pile of garbage.

"Oh, dear. Those sound like teddy bear tears," she said to herself. "I'd better go and see if I can help."

She flew down to take a look, and sure enough, there amongst a heap of old potato peelings and banana skins sat a very old, very sad teddy indeed. Mavis sat and held his paw, while he told her what had happened:

"My owner, Matylda, was told to clean out her room. She's terribly messy, but she's sweet and kind," Teddy sniffed. "She threw me out with an old blanket by mistake — she didn't realise I was tucked up having a sleep inside it. Then some

men in a big dirty truck came and emptied me out of the trash can and brought me here. But I want to go home!" And with that poor Teddy started to cry again.

"There, there," said Mavis. "I'll help to get you home. But first I'll need two teddy bear tears." She unscrewed the lid of a little jar, and scooped two big salty tears into it from Teddy's cheeks.

"What do you need those for?" asked Teddy, feeling rather bewildered.

"Just a little fairy magic!" said Mavis. "Now wait here, and I promise I'll be back soon." And with a wave of her wand she disappeared.

Teddy pulled the blanket around him, and sat trying to be brave, and not to cry. He stayed like that all night, feeling cold and alone and frightened. How he wished he was back in his warm cozy home.

Meanwhile Mavis was very busy. She flew back and forth around the neighborhood, until she heard the sound of sobbing coming from an open window. She flew down onto the window sill and peered inside. A little girl was lying on the bed, with her mommy sitting beside her.

"I want my teddy!" she cried.

"Well if you weren't so messy Matylda, you wouldn't lose things," said Mommy gently.

"But I cleaned my room today!" said Matylda.

"Well, try and go to sleep now," said Mommy, kissing her goodnight, "and we'll look for Teddy in the morning."

Mavis watched as poor Matylda lay sobbing into her pillow, until at last she fell fast asleep. Then Mavis flew down from the window sill, took out the little jar, and rubbed Teddy's tears onto Matylda's sleeping eyes. With a little fizzle of stars, the fairy magic began to work, and Matylda started to dream. She could see an old tire, a newspaper, some tin cans, some orange

peel, a blanket... wait a minute, it was her blanket, and there, wrapped inside it was her teddy, with a big tear running down his cheek! Teddy was at the garbage dump!

The next morning, Matylda woke with a start, and remembered her dream at once. She ran downstairs to the kitchen, where Mommy was making breakfast, and told her all about it.

"We have to go to the garbage dump! We have to save Teddy!" said Matylda.

Mommy tried to explain that it was just a dream, but Matylda wouldn't listen, so in the end they set off to take a look.

They arrived just as a big machine was scooping up the garbage and heading for the crusher. And there, on top of the scoop, clinging to the edge, was Teddy!

Mavis appeared, hovering in the air above him. "Don't worry, we'll save you!" she said. She waved her wand in a bright flash above Teddy. Matylda looked up and spotted him at once.

"There he is!" she cried, pointing frantically at Teddy. "He's going to be squashed! Mommy, do something, quick!" Mommy ran up to the man driving the machine, waving her arms in the air.

He stopped his machine just in time.

Soon Teddy and Matylda were reunited, and there were more tears, although this time they were happy ones. And from then on, Matylda's room was the tidiest room you have ever seen.

THE END